THE PUSHING IN THE POND

BAKERS AND BULLDOG MYSTERIES BOOK 19

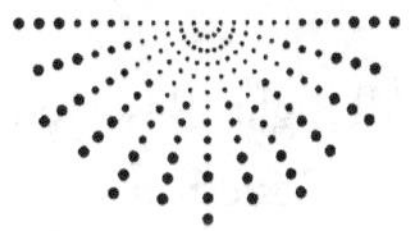

ROSIE SAMS

SWEETBOOKHUB.COM

Rosie is a member of SweetBookHub, a place where you can find amazing fun books that are all sweet and suitable for all ages. Join the exclusive newsletter and get 3 free books here

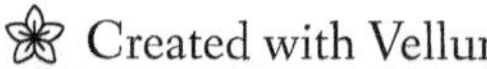
Created with Vellum

Dear reader,

A Graduation Party can end up being deadly. Luckily French Bulldog Smudge and her keeper Melody Marshal are on the case.

It is such an honor to share this book with you. I have always been a fan of three things, my French bulldog, baking, and sweet cozy mysteries.

What could be better than curling up with a dog on your lap, a nice cake at your side, and a cozy mystery to read?

I have recently joined a team of sweet authors at

SweetBookHub.com Grab Smudge and the Stolen Puppies for FREE here

Our aim is to entertain you with sweet books that you will love to read.

I have lots of books out, more to come soon, and two fabulous box sets Cupcakes and Crimes Volume 1 and 2. You can grab the box sets here for free on kindle unlimited or find all my books on Amazon here.

CHAPTER ONE

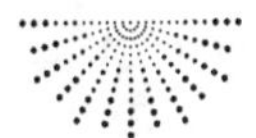

Melody Hennessy stretched as the door closed and the latest customer walked away. Her blue-gray French bulldog, Smudge, was hiding under the counter. As Melody looked down the Frenchie covered her eyes with her paws. Melody couldn't help but giggle. It had been a busy morning for they were in the process of taking orders for the graduation party season. It seemed that everybody wanted to use their bakery and Decadently Delicious was busier than it had ever been.

Kerry Porter-Smedley rushed through from the back room. Her blonde hair was all awry and sneaking out of the bright pink hairnet that she always wore. "Was that another order? she asked.

"It certainly was, how many have we got now?" Melody asked.

"That makes seven. We can manage that many, we can even manage a few more but let's just hope we don't get too many or we will have to be turning customers away." Kerry had obviously had one too many coffees already today, the speed of her speech was faster than a racing train.

Melody held up her hand in surrender. "As long as you let me know if you take any orders without me, I'll keep my eye on it," Melody said. She noticed Leslie, a small exotic woman with a pixie face and dark black hair, was giggling at her from across the room. Leslie was repacking the display case with muffins and cookies before the three partners took a well-earned coffee break.

"Time for a coffee," Kerry said. "I fancy a raspberry and white chocolate muffin, is anyone joining me? Oh, is Lola coming in today?"

"Yes, she should be here any minute now," Melody

blurted out before Kerry could say anymore. "I'll grab the muffins, you get the coffee."

As Melody pulled the muffins out of the cabinets, the doorbell tinkled and Lola came into the shop. Tall and a little too slim and with long black hair, Lola was a pretty woman in her mid-30s. Still a little nervous, her eyes searched the room as she came in. It was an old habit, as a veteran who had been through a lot, she was always looking for danger.

"Hey, Lola you're just in time for a break. Do you fancy a muffin?"

Lola nodded as she walked into the shop. "That sounds great, I'll have what you're having."

"Go on through," Melody said. "Smudge and the girls are in the break room."

Lola lifted the flap and ducked behind the counter disappearing into the back of the bakery while Melody pulled out another muffin.

Soon they were all drinking coffee and eating muffins. Smudge sat on Lola's knee, occasionally giving her kisses or begging for crumbs.

"How are you doing?" Melody asked Lola.

"I'm good. I'm settled in with Jake and we're even thinking about looking for a dog for me."

Smudge gave a little yip and Lola cuddled her close. "Don't worry, Smudge, I'll always love you first."

Smudge grumbled her appreciation as only a Frenchie could. It was a combination of a groan, a grumble, and a whine and made everyone in the room laugh.

"That is really good news," Melody said. "Smudge and I would love to come and help you look."

"And me too," Kerry said.

"And me three," Leslie added with a giggle.

Leslie and Kerry were Melody's partners in the bakery and some time ago Smudge had rescued some Beagle puppies that were stolen. Leslie and Kerry had ended up rescuing two of them each. It had been a while since they had had a puppy play date and Melody thought that maybe it would be a good idea to get everyone together again before Lola left.

Lola hadn't yet decided where she was going once she left Port Warren, but Melody knew that she would be leaving sometime soon and she realized how much she was going to miss her.

"We still haven't picked patterns for the nursery," Kerry said. "It's been a month since I knew about this pregnancy and I feel as if I'm letting you down. I happen to have brought in some books for you to skip through, just hang on while I go fetch them."

Melody and Leslie laughed as Kerry walked over to the counter at the side of the room and pulled down a huge bag. Struggling to hold it she came across to the table and pulled out two massive books.

"Where did you get these?" Melody asked.

"Secrets of the trade," Kerry said. "But I have it on good authority that the majority of patterns you might be interested in will be in here. There is everything from stripes to floral to stars to themes. We have animal themes, space themes, themes from movies, princess themes." She winked. "You tell me what sort of thing you're thinking of and we will find it in here then all we need to do is arrange a day or two to decorate the nursery."

"Whoa! Wait a minute," Melody said. "I can't choose

patterns until we have a gender. Which won't be for another 4 to 5 weeks."

Kerry stopped drinking her coffee, her eyes open wide, looking just like the cartoon on her world's biggest coffee drinker mug. "I can't wait that long! I need to be doing something, to be organizing, to be sorting things out, to be helping, to be doing anything to make sure that this is all going to work out perfectly..."

Everyone at the table except Kerry was laughing.

"You are so mean to me, just because I get excited and talk a little fast." Kerry joined in with the laughter. "Okay, I'll calm down and I'll do things at your pace... I promise."

Melody patted her on the shoulder. "I wouldn't have you any other way Ker, you are a true friend."

Kerry blushed and picking up her coffee mug, she took a big slurp. "Oh, shucks!"

The bell on the store door tinkled and took them all by surprise. Kerry jumped, Leslie laughed, and so did Lola.

"I'll get that," Melody said, "you all enjoy your break."

Melody went through to the shop to see Franklin Reid standing at the counter. He was a tall, distinguished looking man with grey hair and a pasty face. His demeanor was one of authority and Melody recognized him as one of the wealthiest residents of their small town, though she wasn't sure if she'd ever seen him in here before.

"How can I help you, Mr. Reid?"

"Oh, erm, Melody isn't it?" he asked as he stared at the cabinets in front of him.

"Yes, that's correct."

"Well, I was recommended your establishment by several of my daughter's friends' parents. Kirsten is about to graduate as valedictorian of the St. John's school."

Melody recognized the school name and knew that it was the most exclusive school for over a 100 miles in any direction. She nearly let out a whistle but managed to keep her face straight. "Let me congratulate you on your daughter's amazing accomplishment."

"That is very good of you. I plan to thank the school with a sizable donation and have to tell you that Kirsten has been accepted into an Ivy League college come the fall. I imagine my daughter will have the best education possible in her quest to become an architect and I want this party of hers to be something special too. Are you able to arrange that for me?"

Melody nodded. "Of course, we will arrange something worthy of your daughter's achievements, something to celebrate her success and the promise of her future. Do you have any details on numbers in mind?"

"Oh, yes of course." He handed over an extensive list that made Melody's eyes boggle. Maybe they wouldn't be able to take on many more jobs if they were to complete this one.

"Is there a problem?" Franklin asked.

"No, not at all. You have been very detailed and very precise in what you need and I will ensure that your order is fulfilled exactly as you require. Your daughter, as does every child, deserves to celebrate this event. Once more I offer my congratulations."

Franklin smiled and nodded and then turned and left the shop. As he did Kerry, Leslie, and Lola walked through from the back with Smudge in tow.

"Was that Franklin Reid?" Leslie asked.

"Yes it was, he just gave us a massive order for his daughter Kirsten's graduation party."

"Ohh," Kerry said. "I've heard some very worrying things about her graduation."

This was the last thing Melody wanted to hear. Why did trouble always have to find her?

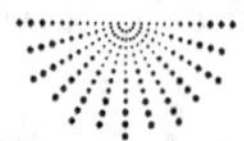

CHAPTER TWO

"We don't need to know this," Leslie said.

Melody could see that Kerry wasn't going to be stopped, she had some information and she would feel bound to let them know. Biting back a sigh, she nodded for Kerry to continue.

"I just heard these rumors about Kirsten," Kerry said. "There are a lot of people saying that she didn't come by her grades honestly and I just wonder whether we should be part of celebrating that?"

For once Kerry had been very brief but it didn't solve Melody's problem. Part of her agreed, if the girl really didn't get her grades honestly should they be helping her celebrate a dishonest effort? However, what could they do? This was gossip and nothing more. She couldn't let idle talk, which could easily be jealousy, get in the way of the task at hand. They were a business and they had to behave professionally. Franklin had hired them to do a job and anything beyond that was none of their business.

"I understand what you're saying, Kerry," Melody said. "However, I don't think this is something we can get involved in. We have to maintain a professional outlook and that doesn't allow us to listen to gossip."

Leslie was nodding her agreement and even though at first, it looked like Kerry might disagree, she too nodded. "I know you're right," Kerry said. "I just think we need to be careful and maybe not advertise the fact that we have taken this order."

"I can understand that," Melody said, "but we're hardly likely to be telling people anyway. Let's just do the best work we can and let everything else take care of itself."

As Leslie and Kerry retired to the kitchen to work on the orders, Lola asked Melody if she cared to take a walk. Melody nodded and shouted in the back to let the girls know. She knew that Lola needed to speak to her and it was something they couldn't talk about in front of her partners.

Fixing a lead to Smudge, Melody grabbed her purse and they set off for a walk. Lola was quiet at first as they walked along the street. Soon, they turned up a leafy path that led to a park. It was a place they enjoyed walking, sitting, and talking. At this time of day, it would be relatively quiet and Lola could say what she needed without anyone hearing.

When they got to the park, Melody let Smudge off her lead. The little blue-gray Frenchie turned to look up at Lola and sat in front of her.

"What's she saying?" Melody asked. Since Lola had told her about her ability to hear animals talk Melody had been obsessed with knowing exactly what Smudge said. Though she believed her relationship with the dog was brilliant, parts of her didn't believe that Lola could really hear the dog talking. Part of her believed it was just residual aftereffects from Lola's head injury, but still, she wanted to know what her little pup was thinking.

"She says I'm looking much better," Lola said.

Smudge did a little yip and spun in a circle before sitting before Lola once more.

"You are looking much better," Melody said. "You are much more relaxed and I think you put a little weight on."

Lola laughed. "I must be the strangest woman because that's good to hear."

Smudge barked again and jumped up at Lola's knees.

"What's the little demanding diva saying now?" Melody asked with a chuckle.

"She wants me to tell you that she loves you and Alvin and she can't wait for the little one to get here."

Melody felt her heart swell with warmth as her hand instinctively went to her stomach. It would be a while before they had a new member of their family but she was so pleased that Smudge was looking forward to it too. "Tell her, I love her too, and that she will always be my favorite little Frenchie."

Smudge gave another bark, spun in a circle in front of Melody, and then raced off across the park.

Lola laughed. "She says she understands you just as you understand her, and blew you a kiss before she went off to investigate."

As they began to walk, they talked of Lola's plans for the future. She still felt as if she had to heal a little bit more before she could set out on her own but each day she was feeling better and stronger. "I think it helped me to know that you and Jake believed in me... or at the very least don't judge me," Lola said.

"I know I didn't know you that well, but I get a gut feeling about these things, and I knew you hadn't killed Elliott Hodge."

"Well, thank you again, thank you for being my friend."

Melody nodded and smiled. "That's easy, you are a good friend of mine too and Smudge is a great reader of character."

Soon Smudge had raced around the park and said hello to everyone she needed to, then she came back and Melody put her on the lead as they prepared to make the return trip to the bakery.

"Do you think there's anything to this gossip?" Lola asked.

"I hope not," Melody said, "but really, it's nothing to do with us so we just have to do the best job we can."

Lola nodded and Melody hoped that it really was nothing to do with them and that there would be no stain on the bakery if Kirsten's deception was found out. As she had that thought, she was mad at herself; here she was believing in gossip when she told others not to.

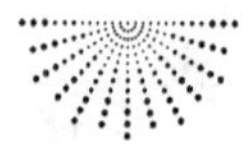

CHAPTER THREE

After a long day at work, Melody and Smudge got home to find her handsome husband and Port Warren's sheriff, Alvin Hennessy, making the dinner. He was stirring one of his famous Cajun chilis and the smell filled the house and made Melody's stomach rumble.

"How was your day?" Alvin asked as he stooped to kiss Melody's cheek.

"It was good, Lola came to see me, we had a nice walk and she told me how much Smudge loves us both and is looking forward to our new little one."

Alvin kissed her lips and ran his hand across her belly. There was hardly a bump as of yet but it still filled her with warmth. At her side, Smudge gave a little bark and scratched at Alvin's legs.

Alvin pulled back and picked up the little bulldog kissing her cheek and rubbing her belly. "I love you too, Smudgeypudgey."

Melody groaned at Alvin's latest attempt to find a nickname, but Smudge just kissed his cheek before wriggling so much that he put her down on the floor. She ran to her bed and grabbed her favorite squeaky green frog toy. Giving it a big squeak, she tossed it into the air and it landed at Alvin's feet.

"I guess that means you're hungry?" Alvin said and turned back to stir the chili in the pan. "Don't worry my two... possibly three... favorite girls, dinner will soon be served."

"Don't get too excited, don't get your hopes up, it might not be a girl," Melody said as she hugged him from behind while he continued to stir the chili.

"I don't care what it is, I don't even care if it's a squeaky frog, it will be our squeaky frog and we will love it just the same."

As if in reply Smudge picked up her own squeaky

frog and ran around the kitchen squeaking in such a frenzy that it filled the house with noise.

Alvin and Melody laughed as they both began to relax into the evening. Soon the table was set, the chili was served, and Smudge had her own meal ready and waiting. As a family, they sat down to eat, and little by little the conversation turned to Melody's day.

"There was one order that is causing a bit of controversy," Melody said.

"Oh good, you know I like controversy." Alvin winked as he grabbed the last piece of garlic bread to clean up the last few smears of chili.

"I'm not so sure you'll like this one," Melody said as she then continued to explain her encounter with Franklin Reid and Kerry's claim that Kirsten had done something underhanded to keep her GPA up.

Alvin chewed his lip for a moment, nodding his agreement. "It might not be all gossip," he said. "I remember a time when Kirsten was seen in the company of a young teaching assistant er... let me think... oh, yes, it was Victor Glass. I remember Wilbur telling me about him. He has this expensive silver lighter and he makes a big show of lighting his slim cigarettes. Wilbur had to ask him to stop once because he was doing it in the movie theater and that was when he noticed that he was with Kirsten. I remember him calling me because she was underage. So, just my thoughts, but this might not all be gossip."

"What happened? Was he…?" Melody couldn't ask any more and she shuddered.

"No, not that we could work out. He said that it was just a treat for her exceptional work, but when I asked around the school they weren't sure what it was for. However, I looked into it and we never saw that they were together again. There was never any evidence of wrongdoing and he was warned about being seen with students. In the end, we couldn't find anything and my gut said he wasn't the sort to abuse her. There was a note made but nothing came of it. Me or one of my officers checked in with him every now and then and nothing… so, who knows?"

"Well, now you've got me thinking." Melody pushed her plate aside and moved her chair back; as she did Smudge jumped up onto her knee. Cuddling the little bulldog close she began to wonder if she should look into this.

"I know that look," Alvin said. "You're thinking of investigating, of poking around to see if you can get to the heart of the matter... don't deny it, I know you too well."

Melody shrugged, she couldn't deny it, it was exactly what she was thinking.

"Please, don't go stirring up trouble, there were never any additional incidents where Kirsten and Victor were seen together so it could've been just a coincidence. There's no reason to spoil the girl's graduation party because of it. Also, the last thing I want is for you to put you and our unborn child at risk by seeking out trouble."

Melody laughed. "Okay, I agree. After all, if there is any trouble you know it will find me."

"Ohh, you are the most stubborn..."

Smudge jumped off Melody's knee and ran around the table. Sitting in front of Alvin she gave a sharp yip. She was obviously taking Melody's side.

"So, now you're ganging up on me," Alvin said while

he tore off a piece of his garlic bread and tossed it at Smudge. The Frenchie jumped into the air and caught the tasty morsel before curling up at his feet and chewing her prize.

"It looks like she forgives you," Melody said, as she hoped Alvin would forgive her if he found out that she started looking into Kirsten's past.

"She always forgives me," Alvin said. "Well, Smudge, just make sure you keep an eye on Melody if and when trouble rears its ugly head again.

Smudge gave a little yip of agreement.

CHAPTER FOUR

The week flew by as a few more graduation party orders came in and Melody, Leslie, and Kerry prepared as many desserts in advance as they could. As often happened, Hiram Green of the Happy Frog restaurant was working on many of the parties as well. This made it doubly easy because they worked well with Hiram, both parties understanding what the other needed.

Melody had made a few discreet inquiries but had found nothing to indicate that Kirsten had done anything untoward. As the day of the party dawned, she put her doubts behind her and looked forward to making it a wonderful event.

The van was packed and soon Melody, Kerry, and

Leslie were unloading and carrying the treats into the Reid's home. Smudge was in the van; Melody had parked it in the shade and the van was refrigerated to keep the desserts cool. Melody was expecting Smudge to stay there for most of the day. She would nip back and make sure that she was okay, giving her plenty of walks in between.

However, Sandra Reid, Franklin's wife, took one look at Smudge and asked if she could get her out of the van. Melody readily agreed and soon Smudge was playing with the family's Pug, a cute little dog called Elvis. It looked like Smudge was certainly going to enjoy the party.

As Melody paused to watch the two dogs race around, she caught a glimpse of a girl standing to one side. Being spotted, the girl nipped behind a big rose bush with the most magnificent candy-striped blooms. The girl was dressed in a beautiful A-Line light pink dress with big pink flowers on it. It was stunning, but it was not the dress that caught Melody's attention. The girl looked nothing short of miserable. It was then that Melody realized she must be the graduate.

Melody looked around and she could see that nobody

seemed to have noticed Kirsten. Putting down her last tray of desserts, Melody crossed the garden and skirted around the rose bush. It was obvious that the girl was hiding, but Melody couldn't leave her in such despair. Slowly, she approached her.

"Hey, I'm Melody, how are you doing?"

Kirsten spun around to face Melody. Long black hair fanned around a pale and tear-stained face. Big brown eyes made her look so young and innocent.

"I didn't mean to startle you," Melody said. "I can understand how overwhelming this party must be; if there's anything I can do just let me know. I know some people don't care for such a fuss as all this."

Melody knew she was talking too much, but her words seemed to relax Kirsten and at last, the girl nodded.

"My parents don't fall into that category," Kirsten said with a shrug. "I didn't really want a party; after all, what is there to celebrate?"

Kirsten's comments made Melody wonder if she was nursing some guilt about her graduation status and her prospects for the future. However, though originally she had wanted to find out some dirt on the girl, now, having met her it was the last thing she wanted.

"Well, I'm happy to lend an ear if you need someone to talk to," Melody said. "It can be just between me and you."

"Thank you for that, I'm not used to people being kind," Kirsten said.

The sound of her mother's voice sharp and commanding rang across the garden. Kirsten jumped.

"Kirsten! Kirsten, get out here and prepare yourself to receive your guests," Sandra bellowed.

Kirsten shrugged once more at Melody before turning and walking away from the rose bush. Melody waited there a moment longer and watched the girl as the guests started to arrive. Once no one was looking in her direction, Melody made her way back to Leslie and Kerry. That was when she noticed Victor Glass coming in.

"The party might prove far more interesting than we expected," Melody whispered to Kerry and Leslie.

Soon the party was in full swing and for a while Melody was busy. Even so, she kept an eye on things and she could see that Franklin and Sandra were basking in the compliments about their daughter's achievements. The school's principal, Richard Jeffries, stated loudly that Kirsten deserved every inch of her success and the wonderful party that celebrated it. However, the guest of honor was nowhere to be seen and Melody started to worry.

Excusing herself, she went out into the back garden and found Smudge, intending to take the bulldog for a walk. Smudge, however, was having so much fun with Elvis, her new friend the pug, that Melody decided to hang outside the house for a few moments. She could keep an eye on the dogs and take in a breath of fresh air.

Stepping around the corner, where it was quieter, she leaned against the wall. It was lovely to watch the two dogs racing around and then flopping down in the grass to rest, before racing around again. Melody wished she had that energy herself as she chuckled at the two pals.

As the dogs took a rest, Melody heard the voices of Kirsten and a young man behind her, the voices were raised and Melody thought about leaving them to it, but instead, she took a few steps closer. There was another rose bush and a large rhododendron between Melody and Kirsten. As Melody peeked through the bushes she could see that it was Victor Glass that Kirsten was arguing with.

Though she wanted to turn away she was drawn to the conversation.

"You would not even have this party had I not intervened on your behalf," Victor said. "I expect you to honor your end of the agreement."

"You did me no favors," Kirsten said before turning and fleeing back to the front door and then, no doubt, back to the party.

Victor shrugged and shook his head. There was a malicious smirk on his face as he pulled a silver lighter from his pocket. With an exaggerated flourish, he lit a slim cigarette and then turned and walked away.

Melody couldn't help herself, she followed, sneaking around the bush she watched as he went through the Reids' gate and approached a pond adjacent to the property. There was something about him that drew her and she decided to casually walk over and say hello. As she skirted the rhododendron, Leslie's voice stopped her dead.

"Are you out here, Melody?"

With one last look at Victor, Melody turned back giving Smudge a quick pat before she went back into the party. Whatever Victor was doing was not her problem and as long as Kirsten was okay she had a job to do.

Still, taking one last glance back she couldn't see Victor through the bushes. She wondered what the man would do? Would he create a scene and spoil this special day?

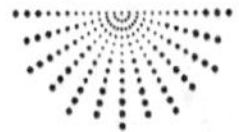

CHAPTER FIVE

Soon the party was in full swing and Melody and her friends were rushed off their feet. As often happened, Hiram Green of the Happy Frog restaurant, was on his own. Melody and her friends helped him serving and preparing food before taking care of their own desserts.

Everyone seemed to be enjoying the party, Franklin and Sandra were basking in the adulation but Melody hadn't seen Kirsten in some time. Part of her wanted to check on the girl but another part of her knew that it was none of her business and maybe she should let her be.

Kerry was drinking cup after cup of strong coffee and

had been dancing with some of the guests as the night carried on. From time to time Melody nipped out and looked after Smudge. The bulldog had had her food and was resting curled up next to Elvis ready for Melody to take her for a walk.

"Just give me five minutes," Melody said, scratching Smudge behind her ears before nipping back inside. Leslie and Kerry had taken a break. Melody took it on herself to tidy up all the empty dishes and to rearrange what food was left. It didn't take her long and she carried the empties back out to the van. That done she decided it was time for Smudge's walk. Grabbing the lead from the van she went back to find Smudge.

When she saw Elvis sitting at Sandra's feet and Smudge nowhere to be found she started to panic. There were some awful tales about dogs being stolen and for a moment her heart was in her throat and she reached for her mobile. Her handsome husband and Port Warren's sheriff, Alvin Hennessy, would be here in an instant if he thought Smudge was in danger. However, before she could dial, she spotted Smudge standing at the Reids' gate.

"What's up, Smudge?" Melody asked.

Smudge spun in a circle and gave a little yip before staring back at the gate. Melody could see that the bulldog's hackles on her back were slightly raised and she was on full alert. Deciding to follow the Frenchie's lead, she clicked the leash to her collar and opened the gate.

Smudge pulled towards the pond and with a chuckle Melody let her lead. Then she recalled seeing Victor Glass standing smoking in that direction. Was he still there? Melody couldn't see him and presumed he had returned back to the party. How she hoped he wouldn't cause any trouble. Though Kirsten hadn't been at her party much Melody didn't think she deserved any scandal.

"Steady," Melody said as Smudge pulled her down towards the water. "You can't need to drink, there was plenty out for you."

Smudge gave a little yip and pulled forward sniffing along the edge of the bank. It was dark and the moonlight glinted off the water. Melody found herself thinking what a romantic place it would be to have a picnic and she wondered if she could persuade Alvin to join her one night.

"What do you think, Smudge?" she asked.

Smudge whined and pulled her right to the water's edge. The little bulldog was sniffing left and right, left and right, and then with a determination, she set off to the left.

Melody always trusted Smudge but now the lake no longer seemed romantic but a little isolated. Though she could still hear the music from the party it was muffled and the lake was so secluded no one would be able to see her. Turning, she tried to guide the bulldog back to the party.

Smudge was having none of it and pulled her around the lake. Melody was always so surprised at how much strength the little dog had when she was determined. The ground was a little slippery, the grass short and it gave her little purchase in the neat black shoes she always wore when on a job. Suddenly, Smudge stopped.

"About time," Melody said. "You really can be a naughty little girl at times."

With a chuckle, she noticed that Smudge was staring down at the water. Looking into the silvery depths herself, Melody suddenly understood. Surely, this couldn't be happening; something was in the water and she soon worked out what it was. As a ray of moonlight touched the surface, Melody let out a high-pitched scream.

CHAPTER SIX

Pushing aside the thought, *not again,* Melody once more reached for her phone. This time she dialed home and Alvin answered almost immediately. Quickly, Melody explained what she had found and Alvin told her he would be there very soon.

"I think you should go back to the party," Alvin said.

Melody shook her head, though she knew he could not see it down the phone. "I should stay here, we don't want anyone messing with... well, with the body."

"I would much rather they mess with the body then

mess with you," Alvin said. "You would be much safer back at the party, just hang on a moment."

Melody heard him put her on hold and knew that he would be calling the station, she also knew he would already be on his way and it would only take him a few minutes to get here. Smudge was at her feet for the moment, but she whined and pulled as if she too wanted to go back to the party. "Wait just a minute," Melody said to the dog just as Alvin came back on the line.

"I can't hear people, are you back at the party?"

"No, not yet."

"We'll do it now, for me, please, and for our child."

Melody chuckled at his concern already. "Okay, I will go back to the party, but if anyone sees me coming back from here, I may even be in more danger?"

Melody heard Alvin draw in his breath and the cruiser he was driving speed up.

"I'll be there any minute, go back and be with Kerry and Leslie but don't tell them anything. If anyone asks you just say you were walking Smudge and nothing else. I love you."

Before Melody could say the words back she knew that Alvin had hung up and that he would be here any minute. Feeling nervous, she glanced around but there was no movement and surely, Smudge would have let her know if anyone was there. "Come on, pup, let's get back to the party," Melody said as she turned to walk away. At first, she wondered if Smudge might be difficult. When the little Frenchie had her nose on the clues it was hard to get her to back down, but to her surprise Smudge turned and walked back as if nothing had happened.

Melody was soon back through the gate and into the garden. There was no one around on that side of the house and as she turned the corner she watched to see if anyone was looking. Making out that she was looking for Kerry and Leslie she scanned the crowd, but no one seemed to be staring at her. With a sense of relief, she spotted Leslie and made her way across.

"Where's Kerry?" Melody asked, suddenly worried for her friend and partner.

"She's over there, dancing, look." Leslie pointed

across the crowded garden and into the dining room. Sure enough, Kerry was bopping away to the music along with half a dozen other people.

"Are you okay?" Leslie asked. "You look as white as a sheet."

Melody let out a breath and shook her head. "Let's just say I will be seeing my husband sooner than I expected."

"Oh, no, not really?" Leslie asked.

Before Melody could say anymore Alvin arrived and Melody watched as he weaved his way through the crowd to get to her. As he pulled her into his arms she saw Wilbur coming in and knew that he would be coming over too.

Alvin held her close and then whispered in her ear, "are you all right?"

"I'm in better shape than Victor Glass," Melody said with a shrug.

"I'm sorry, that was a silly thing to ask. Can you point me in the right direction and I will go check things out. I'm hoping to bring a team around the back so that we can question some of the people and watch their reaction before we make an announcement."

Melody pulled back from him and took his hand in hers. "It will be easier if I just show you."

Wilbur was now next to Leslie, holding her hand. Alvin nodded to Wilbur as Melody led him away from the party.

Soon, Melody had led Alvin back to the pond. All the time, Smudge was pulling to go back to the party.

"Is she trying to tell us something?" Alvin asked.

"It's possible," Melody said, "however, she met a pug called Elvis and I'm pretty sure the two of them are in love." Melody was surprised that she gave a chuckle at the thought of the two dogs. Was she getting so used to murder or was it just the need to have a little bit of normality under such terrible circumstances?

They made their way around the pond and Alvin got her to stand back while he went to look at the body. He squatted down on his knees and searched the riverbank, but he was careful not to touch the body or to destroy any evidence. Before he came back to her he called in on his radio and walked away in the opposite direction just a short distance so that he could guide his crew directly to the pond.

The coroner's wagon was the first to arrive and behind them the crime scene team. Once Alvin had organized his people he returned to Melody.

"I can get Wilbur to drive you and the girls home," Alvin said.

"I'm not sure about them," Melody said, "but I'd like to stay." As they walked back to the party she explained about Kirsten being miserable and how she had seen Victor smoking, and then about how the girl's parents didn't seem to care that she was miserable.

"It seems like a really nice family," Alvin said.

Melody knew that at one time she wanted to stop the party and to shame Kirsten if she were guilty, but now, she just hoped the young girl would be okay.

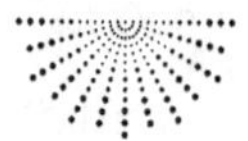

CHAPTER SEVEN

More officers had arrived and Melody noticed deputy John Peterson standing to one side with two other officers. She had only met him a couple of times and she could see he was nervous. A recent new recruit, the young officer of color had always greeted her with a smile. When he caught her eye, she gave him a nod and a smile and was relieved to see him relax.

Alvin approached the officers.

"I'll speak to Kerry and Leslie," Melody said.

Alvin nodded and continued to the officers. Melody knew that he would seal off the house to prevent anyone from leaving and then start asking questions. Weaving her way through the crowd she soon found Leslie and was not surprised to see that Kerry was with her.

"Have you really done it again?" Kerry asked. "We can't ever have a night off without you finding a body!"

"Shush!" Leslie said, holding her hand up and looking around the room nervously.

"Well, I'm right," Kerry said, and then she seemed to sag. Her shoulders drooped and all the energy went out of her face.

"It looks like you need a coffee," Melody said and guided the two girls into the kitchen. It was quiet there. The only other person in the large and beautifully appointed room was Hiram Green.

"Hey, ladies, how are you doing?" Hiram asked.

Melody shut the door and gestured for him to join them. "Did you leave the house at all?" Melody asked Hiram.

"No, I've been hiding in here most of the night.

Felicity Parker seems to have taken a shine to me," Hiram said.

Leslie chuckled. "I saw her earlier, I didn't realize she was chasing you."

"It was most embarrassing; I've been hiding behind that door for the better part of an hour." Hiram shrugged and Leslie and Kerry laughed a little too heartily. "What's wrong, Melody?" Hiram asked.

Turning away for just a moment Melody grabbed four mugs and poured them all a coffee. She would not normally be drinking anything with caffeine at this time of night but somehow she thought she would need to be awake for a few hours yet. Handing out the mugs she guided them across to a large kitchen table. Once they all sat down she explained what had happened.

"Alvin has said that you and Kerry can leave if you want to," Melody said, "sorry, Hiram, I think he might want to question you."

Hiram shrugged. "It's okay, I don't need to rush back."

"I'm okay to stay too," Leslie said.

Kerry nodded her agreement. "It looks like you've done most of the clearing up, Melody. Leslie and I can finish that off and then we may as well hang around until this is all over. It would look kinda wrong if we left when others can't."

Melody was very proud of her partners. "Thank you, all of you. Why don't you stay in here, you will be out of the way and I'll go see what Alvin's up to."

Melody and Smudge left the kitchen and she could see that Alvin and Wilbur were questioning the party guests. Melody went across to Alvin and stood slightly behind him. Everyone he spoke to was saying they knew nothing, had seen nothing. It looked like it was going to be a long night!

Melody tapped Alvin on the shoulder and guided him to a quiet spot. "Did I mention that Victor and Kirsten were fighting earlier?" Melody asked. She knew she had intended to but wasn't sure if she got around to it before they were back at the party. Finding a body could be enough to put you off your train of thought.

"No, you said you saw him smoking."

"I'm sorry, Alvin, he went off for a smoke after he was arguing with Kirsten. He said something along the lines of, I expect you to honor your end of the agreement. Kirsten then replied that he did her no favors, before storming away. I don't think it could've been her, as I don't think she could have got past me and committed the crime and then got back to the party."

"Well, we'll bear that in mind. I was just about to start interviewing the family."

As he said that Smudge started to bark and was pulling on her lead.

"Shush, Smudge," Melody said casting her eye at where the bulldog was looking. It was at the Reid family group and noticed that Kirsten was there. There were a couple of other girls' parents and Principal Jefferies. Melody couldn't help but notice that they all seemed uneasy.

Alvin glanced down at Smudge and then led the way over to the Reids. "Mr. and Mrs. Reid, folks." Alvin nodded to the group. "Kirsten, I would like to interview you next, if you will come this way with me."

Franklin stepped forward. "You cannot talk to my daughter alone, she is a minor and one of her parents needs to be present for any kind of interrogation."

"I wasn't planning on interrogating her, Mr. Reid, merely asking her a few questions."

Franklin moved between Alvin and his daughter. "Even so, I would like to be there."

Kirsten stepped around him. "You are forgetting, Father, that I have just turned 18. Sheriff Hennessy, I am happy and willing to talk to you on my own, please follow me to my room."

"Kirsten, do you mind if I tag along?" Melody asked.

"Not at all, you have been nice to me this evening... which is more than a lot of people have," Kirsten said before turning and walking away.

Alvin raised his eyebrows at Melody and then followed her as they made their way through the house. At first, they were weaving through crowds but then they went through a door into a quiet corridor. It was painted in a light ash color with large photos on either side. Melody noticed that they were not of the family, and she thought that strange. It was almost too perfect, like a corridor in a high-end hotel.

Kirsten opened a door and invited them into her bedroom. It was a nice sized room, decorated in peach. There were no photos or posters of boys on the walls and very little about the room looked personal to Kirsten. The bed was on one side and on the other side in front of a desk was a small sofa, a coffee table, and two chairs. There was a book on car engines on the bed.

"I feel happy to talk in here if that's okay with you?" Kirsten asked. "It's the one place we won't be disturbed."

"If you're comfortable here, we are fine," Melody said as she sat in one of the chairs. Smudge sat down on the floor next to her.

Alvin took the other and Kirsten nodded and went around the table and sat on the sofa. With her hands on her knees and her back straight, she looked most uncomfortable. Melody noticed that she was chewing her lip and she wanted to put her at ease.

"Don't worry," Melody said, "we just want to ask you a few questions."

"I'm not quite sure what to say," Kirsten said. "I'm not used to people dying."

"As Melody said, there's nothing to worry about," Alvin added. "I just want to ask you what your relationship with Victor was?"

Kirsten's eyes opened wide and she shook her head vehemently. "There was nothing dirty about it."

"We didn't say there was," Melody said quickly and she noticed the girl relax just a little bit. "How well did you know him?"

Kirsten sighed. "I was foolish enough to trust him with a secret, once."

Melody felt her senses come on high alert. Maybe she had been wrong, maybe Kirsten was involved. "What secret?"

"I told him about my parents' desires for my future and how much they wanted it. I wish I hadn't and that is all... I swear to you."

"I believe you," Melody said. "However, I heard you arguing with him earlier. It sounded like there was more to it than that. It sounded like he was bribing you."

Kirsten swallowed. "I don't know what he did... or if he did anything. However... Victor claimed that he used his position at the school to alter some of my final marks. I never asked him to. I never wanted him to. It wasn't my dream to go to college." She raised her arms in the air. "None of this is my dream."

"I understand," Melody said.

Smudge gave a little whine and walked across the room. Sitting beside Kirsten she rubbed her head on her leg.

"Unfortunately, your confession will prompt the school to cast a closer eye on your graduating class," Alvin said.

"I don't care," Kirsten said and Melody believed her. "I'm open to any investigation, the truth might even set me free. I don't know what else I can tell you, I've been here in my room most of the night."

"That's okay, that's all we need for now," Alvin said and started to stand.

"What about any of the other graduates, would they want an investigation?" Melody asked.

"I'm sure they wouldn't," Kirsten said. "Especially

Mary Brigg's parents. They stood next to my parents. Mary wants college so much and I'm not sure that she has what it takes..." Kirsten's words drifted off and she looked down, once more miserable and maybe feeling guilty at telling on the other girl.

"Thank you for your help," Melody said, "if you think of anything more give us a call."

Kirsten nodded and then leaned back on the sofa and grabbed hold of a fluffy peach cushion. She hugged it to her chest as they left the room.

Alvin, Melody, and Smudge walked along the corridor.

"I wonder if she might have pushed Victor to trigger that investigation?" Alvin asked.

"I'm not so sure," Melody said. "After all, Smudge liked her and I get the feeling there's more to the story than what we've heard. I think we should question Franklin and Sandra and the Briggs before coming to a final decision. And then, there's always other graduates. If there was some impropriety going on I'm sure it wouldn't just be Kirsten's grades."

Alvin nodded. "You are probably right, I just feel

that she is hiding something... and anyone who is hiding something... is always a suspect in my book."

Melody chuckled. "Everyone's a suspect in your book."

Smudge gave a little yip of agreement.

CHAPTER EIGHT

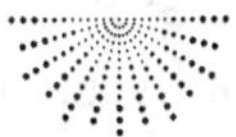

As they re-entered the main part of the house the noise of so many voices was playing on Melody's nerves. Everyone was chatting, talking, and almost shouting to be heard. Smudge gave a little whine, pulled on her lead, and seemed to be searching the room.

"Are you looking for your friend?" Melody asked.

Smudge gave a little bark and then pulled them through the crowd.

"What's wrong with her?" Alvin asked.

Melody gave a little chuckle. "She's either looking for Elvis or she's hot on a clue. Should we follow her?"

"Well, I want to question Franklin and Sandra next, I asked the deputies to leave them to me." Alvin scanned the room. "I can't see them yet, so we may as well follow her and see if we find them."

Melody loosened her grip a little and started to follow Smudge. She could see the deputies. Each one was in a separate area of the room and each was questioning one or more people. They passed through room after room until they came to the large games room area that opened onto the garden. Smudge was still leading and she led them straight to Franklin and Sandra who were stood with the Briggs and Principal Jefferies. This group were as thick as thieves.

Sitting down in front of them, Smudge gave a little whine and Melody wondered if she really was missing Elvis or if this was something more. Looking around, she hadn't seen the pug and for a moment she wondered where he was. Alvin's questions pulled her mind back to the present.

"We would like to ask you some questions now if you don't mind," Alvin said.

"Of course not," Sandra said but Melody noticed

that Franklin stiffened. He was not happy about answering questions.

"We will leave you to it," Mr. Briggs, a large, red-faced man said as the rest of the group evaporated into the crowd.

"Did you leave the house at all during the party?" Alvin asked.

Sandra shook her head. "No, we have been so busy. Everyone wanted to congratulate us and if we were to leave it would look very strange."

Melody bit her lip. They were so busy that they hadn't noticed their daughter's misery or that she was missing from her own party. "I imagine you spent a lot of time with Kirsten too," Melody said, hiding her sarcasm only slightly.

Alvin kicked her ankle and she coughed to cover the little squeal she almost made.

Alvin asked a few more questions about who they had spoken to, at what time, and if they'd seen anyone else leave the party. Melody knew what he was doing. These were easy questions to get them to talk and to open up. Once he believed that they had let down their guard he would ask something a little bit more pressing.

"I hear that Victor Glass was instrumental in altering your daughter's final grades," Alvin said the words so matter of factly that they would often fall beneath people's radar. It didn't work!

Color rose up Franklin's neck, across his cheeks, ears, and out through his forehead. Melody could almost imagine steam coming out of his nose he seemed so enraged. At his side, his fists were clenched and his teeth were gritted.

Alvin remained calm, this change of attitude would tell him a lot. For a moment, Melody thought that Franklin would lose control completely. That he would fly at Alvin, fists first. Instead, he seemed to bite back his anger. Dropping his gaze, he shook his head and then raised his eyes to Alvin.

"I do not believe a word of this. I do not like to speak ill of the dead but the man was a worm. He was always looking for something and someone to blame for the lack in his life. If anything, he was using my daughter's success to try and bolster his own career. Who knows if he did that to somebody else? Maybe that is where you should look for your murderer. Mary Briggs would never get good grades, I suggest you check hers! As I said, I had no contact with Victor Glass."

At that moment Melody noticed that Kerry, who had been cleaning up the tables and the mess from the party, had stopped behind them. In her normal bold way, she pushed in between the group of people. "But that's funny because I saw you two arguing earlier," Kerry said, and then she turned to Melody and Alvin. "I couldn't hear exactly what they were saying but things were definitely heated." Kerry turned back to Franklin. "So, what have you got to say about that then?" she asked before walking away.

Melody had to bite back a chuckle, Kerry was all tact.

"I have nothing to say to that," Franklin said. "In fact, I have no intention of saying anything else without the benefit of my lawyer's presence."

Alvin nodded. "That is indeed your right, but understand I will do everything in my power to investigate this murder. It doesn't matter where the clues lead, I will follow them and at the moment, this house is part of the crime scene. You don't have to answer my questions at this minute, but just make sure you don't leave town, we will be speaking again."

As they started to turn, Melody noticed that Smudge was pulling on her lead again. Thinking that she was still looking for the pug Melody tried to bring her with them. Smudge had other ideas, she went with them for a moment, easing the pressure on the lead, and then she turned and ran tugging the lead through Melody's fingers.

The little Frenchie ran straight to Sandra, sitting in front of her and starting to whine. Sandra smiled down at Smudge and as she was about to stroke her Franklin took her hand and pulled her away.

Smudge sat and watched them go, whimpering a little before turning and trotting back to Melody.

"What do you make of that?" Alvin asked.

Melody shook her head, she wasn't sure. Was Smudge simply drawn to the lady of the house because she wanted to play with Elvis again, was she comforting her, or did Sandra know more than what she was saying? Had Smudge witnessed something while playing with the Reids' pug?

After a few more interviews, Alvin and Melody made their way over to the Briggs family. Melody knew that Alvin had not gone straight to them on purpose. He was letting them sweat, if they were guilty, the longer it took for an interview the more worked up they would be. Alvin had let them notice him looking at them as he made his way around the party.

Turning over a page in his notepad with exaggerated care Alvin fixed his gaze on Mr. Briggs. The portly man went even redder. The blue veins on his bulbous nose spoke of his affinity for alcohol and Melody wondered if this was in fact their killer. Smudge stood at her side, the lead loose paying him no attention.

"Mr. Briggs, I heard a rumor that Victor Glass altered your daughter's grades. What do you say to that?" Alvin went straight in for the kill. Having watched the man he would alter his interrogation technique to get the most out of that question and this worked. Mr. Briggs was shaking, only soon the anger turned to a laugh and both Melody and Alvin took a step back.

"Do you care to explain your amusement?" Alvin asked.

"Well, if I paid Victor to alter young Mary's grades I didn't get much for my money," he said and rubbed the top of his daughter's head. She was a sweet-looking girl, a little plain but she seemed happy. She was not quite what Melody had expected.

"Please explain," Melody said.

"Well, we were just like the Reids, pushing our daughter to be what we wanted and making her mean and unhappy. Finally, she sat down and spoke to us and said she didn't want to go to college. That was when we realized what we had done. You can check Mary's grades, we are proud of them, but they wouldn't be worth killing for."

Alvin asked a few more questions but Melody knew these people weren't the killer; after all, Smudge had ignored them.

Melody and Alvin watched the Briggs's walk away. "It could still be them," Alvin said.

"How do you get that?" Melody asked.

"Well, if they paid for good grades and got poor ones they have a motive."

Melody groaned and Alvin laughed.

"Okay, I do tend to see everyone as a suspect. I think maybe they didn't do it but let's not rule them out just yet."

Melody smiled and leaned against him as they shared a moment of privacy before returning to questioning the guests.

It was a few days later and Melody, Leslie, and Kerry were all taking a coffee break. They had worked hard all morning and the shop had been particularly busy. Luckily, at last, it had gone quiet and so they took the time to sneak into the break room and have a coffee and a chocolate chip muffin.

"How's the case going?" Kerry asked before taking another sip of her coffee. For once her sentences seemed about the same as everyone else's. Maybe because this was her first coffee break in a few hours and she needed her breath to inhale the hot beverage.

Melody let out a long sigh. "Alvin is no closer to

making an arrest at the moment. While both Franklin and Kirsten have a motive for the murder, no one at the party recalls seeing either of them leaving the premises. My gut says it's not Kirsten... but maybe I just feel sorry for her."

"Me too," Leslie said. "As in, I feel sorry for her. It was very busy at that party, the lack of a solid eyewitness means nothing."

"She's right," Kerry said joining the conversation with gusto. "There were so many guests at the party. Everyone was milling around this way and that way talking and laughing and joking and dancing. Going from room to room and back again. It would be impossible for people to keep track of one another. Who knows who went where and for how long?"

Melody held up her hand but it wouldn't stop Kerry when she was in full flow.

"All I'm saying is the lack of a witness doesn't prove anything. It just means no one saw them leave, not that they didn't leave.

"You are right," Melody said. "I'm still suspicious of Sandra. I don't know why but I know there is something that she is not saying. Who knows, maybe

Franklin's desire to lawyer up was to protect his wife and not himself."

"I know that look," Leslie said, "what are you going to do?"

Melody laughed. Her friend was right, she did have an idea. "I think I might head back to the Reids' and try to talk to Sandra. Who knows, I might find something out!"

"No," Leslie said.

"She's right, Mel. That's not a good idea, especially not in your condition. You know, being pregnant and all. You need to take extra special care and you don't want to be getting involved with any murderers. Alvin would kill us if we let you get hurt."

Melody laughed. "I really appreciate your concern, but I'm not going to get hurt. I'll have Smudge with me and I can still take care of myself. I even have a good excuse."

"What's that?" Leslie asked.

"I'm bringing Smudge for a play date with Elvis. Sandra really loved to see the two dogs play, I'm sure she'll be delighted to see me." Melody hoped this would be the case, for the last thing she wanted at the moment was any trouble.

Melody made the short drive to the Reids' house and was soon pulling up outside. Fixing a lead onto Smudge's collar she made her way to the door and knocked, in what she hoped was a friendly fashion. *Was that even possible?*

Sandra opened the door with Elvis, the pug, at her feet. The two dogs were delighted to see each other, wiggling and doing little barks and yips but Sandra seemed less than happy. The scowl on her face told Melody that she was not welcome.

"I'm here alone, what do you want?" Sandra asked.

"I was just passing and I knew Smudge and Elvis would love to play so I just thought I'd see if you were doing all right. Or if you need anything?"

Sandra hesitated for a few moments but as Smudge started to whimper, she opened the door and let them in. "Franklin and Kirsten were called to a meeting with Principal Jeffries. They are discussing Kirsten's graduation status... Franklin thought it best if I stay here."

Melody found that highly suspicious. *What is Sandra hiding?*

"Come on through, and I'll make a coffee, the dogs can run around in the garden," Sandra said.

Melody followed them through and Sandra poured 2 cups of coffee and offered Melody a cookie from a tray. Had she been alone or were they for someone else?

Sandra was about to lead her outside when she turned around to find Smudge standing on her hind legs and waving her paws in front of her. Sandra's eyes grew wide as if she was frightened and Melody's suspicions kicked up another notch. Thinking it was now or never, Melody decided to press the point.

"That is terrible," Melody said offering a little sympathy to start. "However, I did hear Victor speaking to Kirsten, the words he was saying were far from kindly. Maybe he had a point?"

Sandra sank down into a chair. It was as if the weight of the world had become too much for her and she had succumbed under the pressure. Smudge gave a little yip and ran out of the room.

Melody walked around the table and pulled out the opposite chair. Placing her cup on the surface Melody waited for Sandra to continue. The seconds stretched and while Melody waited Smudge appeared back in the room. The little bulldog walked up to Sandra and rested her head against her leg. Her offer of comfort confused Melody. One moment ago, she seemed suspicious now, rather than play with the pug, she was here offering support! It was almost enough to make her believe that Sandra was innocent. But still, she waited and let the silence speak for her. For long moments the seconds ticked by, but Melody had watched the best in her husband, Alvin, and she knew to wait Sandra out. Silence could be deafening when you had a guilty conscience.

Eventually, Sandra let out a sigh and her eyes raised to meet Melody's. "I may as well tell you... because the sheriff is bound to find out eventually. I overheard the same conversation and I raced after the teaching assistant."

"I didn't see you," Melody said though she wished she hadn't.

"There is another gate behind the topiary hedge. It is very secluded and hard to find. No one would see anyone leaving that way... but I swear to you that all I did was offer Victor a bribe. I just wanted to keep him quiet. Only it wasn't that easy, he said that he didn't want a one-time payment. What he wanted was for me to pay him monthly and for me to put in a good word for him with Principal Jeffries. Victor wanted to secure a tenured position on the teaching staff." Sandra paused and took a big gulp of her coffee. It was strange to see this small and pristine woman drinking with as much finesse as a member of a chain gang.

Once more, Melody waited but she did give Sandra a nod of encouragement to continue.

"I could have given him a one-off payment, but there is no way I could manage continuous payments, certainly not without Franklin finding out. I guess I was a little horrified at the man's awful treatment of both me and my daughter. In tears, I fled back to

Franklin and filled him in on the complete conversation."

Now it was getting interesting. "I understand," Melody said. "I hate that Victor did that to you, it must've been awful and I understand how you feel. Do you think that Franklin might have opted for violence... as a way to eliminate Victor's threat?"

As Melody watched, Sandra seemed to shrink even more. The posture said more than words but soon her words confirmed Melody's fears.

"I don't want to say..." Tears fell from her eyes and she looked devastated.

"These things will come out, tell me what it is you're worried about," Melody said and reached out a hand to offer comfort.

"I'm sad to admit this... but I'm not sure. I love my husband and my daughter but they were acting strangely after the party. They kept their eyes on one another all the time. Something felt off to me."

Melody felt as if she had got what she needed. Franklin was the obvious candidate and if his own wife suspected him, then all Melody had to do was find the evidence to prove this theory. However, there was still something about Sandra that made her think she was more involved than she was letting on. It hadn't taken much for Melody to get her to blame her husband and that didn't sit well with Melody. However, Smudge was still offering Sandra her comfort. The Frenchie was a good judge of character and Melody nearly scratched Sandra off the suspect list — nearly.

As they said their goodbyes one thing was for certain, Melody was still no closer to identifying Victor's killer.

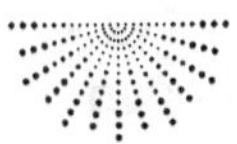

CHAPTER TEN

Melody made her way back to the car, fastening Smudge into her harness and attaching it to the safety belt. Smudge must have seen Sandra with Victor before she fled in tears. It was just something that the bulldog was keyed into. Melody wondered if Smudge then kept an eye on Victor. Possibly noticing him go to the bank of the pond. If she had, she must've seen the person who actually pushed Victor into the water. There was no doubt in Melody's mind that Smudge would growl at the individual. The only problem was, Smudge hadn't growled at any of her suspects.

The day was drawing in and Melody wondered if the girls had already left the shop. They had a graduation party, but this was a small one and it was Melody's night off. She and Kerry would do the next one and she and Leslie the one after. Work was very busy and a little hard at the moment; luckily, they all loved what they did.

As she drove, Melody began to think of all the people who could have a motive to kill Victor. There were, of course, other parents, and possibly other people at the school. If it had leaked out that Victor had been telling the truth then scandal would follow.

Melody pulled her car into the back of the bakery and could see that the van was missing. Grabbing her keys from her purse she released Smudge and stepped around to the front door. It was getting late, and officially they should be closed, but Melody had a few jobs she wanted to do before she went home. So, she may as well open up.

Walking in she went under the counter and unlocked the door, turning the sign to open. Then she found a butter cookie for Smudge on a note from Leslie.

We cleaned up for you.

I hope you solved the crime.

Have a great evening, see you tomorrow.

Leslie and Kerry

xoxo

Melody tossed the butter cookie to Smudge, who grabbed it and ran out of the room and into the break room to her bed. Melody smiled as she knew that Smudge would eat it there before being ready to leave. She was about to pick up her purse to go to her office and check tomorrow's workload when the door opened and Principal Jeffries walked in.

"Melody, isn't it?" he asked.

"That's right, how can I help you?"

"I was just surprised to see you open... I was just walking past. I wondered if I might purchase some of your wonderful profiteroles? I enjoyed them so much at Kirsten's party that I just had to take some home."

Melody smiled. "Just give me a moment and I'll check if we have any left. Melody walked through into the kitchen and opened the fridge. Sure enough, there was one portion of profiteroles left. Quickly, she boxed them up before returning to the shop.

"You are in luck," she said and then stopped instantly. Smudge stood behind the counter, her hackles raised and a growl coming from deep within her little throat. *How do I always get into these situations*, Melody thought?

On alert, Melody scanned her late customer. He would've had a reason to want to keep Victor quiet, but would he want him dead? Melody knew she stood staring but for some reason, she couldn't move as all the possibilities ran through her mind. If Victor really had messed with Kirsten's grades, it did not reflect well on the school. What would the principal do to keep Victor silent? Of course, he could've been bribed in the same way Sandra was. Would he push Victor into the pond to save himself the financial burden?

"Are you all right?" Richard Jeffries asked. "You've gone as white as a sheet and your dog appears to dislike me."

Melody watched his face change. So far, he had looked dignified and pleased to see her but the realization now struck him and it changed his persona completely. The man before her most definitely looked like someone who could kill. He was certainly someone who would not take prisoners and he would want the likes of Victor out of the way. Deciding that her best bet was to meet him head-on Melody swallowed and cleared her throat.

"You forget, Richard, that my dog was at the party. She smelt whoever committed the crime and I think she just worked out who that was." As imperceptibly as she could Melody reached into her pocket for her phone. She could speed dial Alvin without looking and that was what she did.

Smudge still stood in front of her, guarding her from the man she knew was a threat.

Richard smirked. "I think you would be better sticking to baking then crime detection. Your profiteroles are delightful but your theory on crime is interesting at best and insulting at worst. Apart from which I had no beef against Victor, none at all. I looked into Kirsten's grades and I found no improprieties. I have to assume that either Kirsten and her father were lying or that Victor was all talk. Either way, all I would have done was sack the man and adjusted Kirsten's grades if need be.

Melody could hear the slight ring tone from her

pocket and then Alvin's answer. She could tell he was talking but she couldn't make out a word. How she hated to scare him in this way, but she also knew that he would be racing towards her as fast as he could. She just hoped that he would be in time.

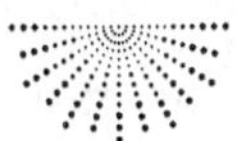

For a moment or two Principal Jeffries and Melody locked eyes. Between them, the little bulldog was growling menacingly and Melody knew that she would not let him near her. However, she also knew that Smudge was so small and she hated the thought of her getting hurt. Maybe if she kept her cool the principal would leave and Alvin could deal with him later.

Smudge turned and yipped at Melody. It was almost as if she was saying don't let him leave, but for once, Melody was more worried about facing down the large man than solving the crime.

"Well, I hope that has cleared that up," Principal

Jeffries said as he reached out for the profiteroles. "Now, how much do I owe you for these?"

Melody shook herself and handed over the box, placing a smile on her face she shook her head. "No charge, it's the end of the day and they are all we had left and after all, I was just rather rude to you."

"Think nothing of it," he said and with a wave, he turned to leave. "Thank you for these, I'll be back for more soon."

Before Melody could stop her, Smudge ran under the counter and in front of him. Leaping forward, she grabbed his trousers by the ankle and shaking and pulling she forced him to the ground. The box of profiteroles flew out of his hand and across the shop as did a certain silver cigarette lighter.

Melody gasped when she realized it was Victor's lighter and that he had it with him before he went to the pond. It was circumstantial but it pointed firmly in the direction of Richard being the killer.

"Control that damn dog," Richard cried as he tried to kick out at Smudge. The Frenchie was darting around him yapping and barking at his ankles.

At last, Melody reached down to pull her phone out of her pocket the sound of sirens came through the phone as she held it to her ear. "Alvin, I'm at the bakery and I have a suspect."

"Hey, Mel. It's so good to hear your voice. I was worried for a moment, how are you doing?"

"I'm okay," she managed.

"Just hold on, I'm nearly there," Alvin said.

"You should've told him who it was," Richard Jeffries said as he dodged Smudge and leaped to his feet. With a face like thunder, he turned towards her and crossed the shop surprisingly quickly for such a large man.

"Alvin, the murderer is Principal Richard Jeffries, he had Victor's lighter in his pocket and he is now threatening me."

There was no answer on the phone but the sound of squealing tires and sirens was suddenly outside the shop. The noise was deafening, as Smudge's barks and growls got louder to compete with the sirens. Before Richard could take another step Alvin raced through the door and grabbed him by the shoulder. Spinning him around.

"You made a big mistake when you threatened my wife," Alvin said as he slapped the cuffs on the man and then handed him to Wilbur who was just coming in the door behind him.

Alvin ran to Melody and pulled her into his arms. It felt wonderful to fall into his strong and safe embrace and she leaned against him until they heard a little bark at their side and felt scratching on their legs. Pulling apart they chuckled as they looked down to see Smudge. Alvin scooped her into his arms and they shared a family cuddle.

Wilbur was holding onto Jefferies. "What am I arresting him for?" Wilbur asked.

Melody pointed to the lighter.

"Ahh, I see," Wilbur said.

"The lighter proves nothing," Jeffries claimed. "Many people have silver lighters and even if it would prove to be Victor's who says he didn't give it to me or I found it?"

Melody could tell that he was rambling now,

struggling to say anything to prove his innocence. It was something she had seen a lot and it made her feel good because she knew they were close. This case would be closed very soon.

"All of that is true," Alvin said. "However, no lighter was found on Victor's body or around or in the pond." He sauntered over to the lighter and taking an evidence bag picked it up and inspected it in front of him. Taking his time, he turned it over in his hands and then turned his gaze onto the principal.

That gaze was enough to make Melody swoon but it had the opposite effect on the bad guys. It made them quake at the knees in a quite different way.

"I find it rather strange that you have a lighter bearing Victor's initials!" Alvin said.

"I found it," Jeffries said.

"Where did you find it?" Melody asked.

"It was on a table at the party."

"Really, because I saw him with it not long before I found him dead," Melody said.

Smudge gave a very self-satisfied little bark and sat down in front of Melody.

Principal Jeffries seemed to crumble. "I only went to the pond to try to reason with Victor, just as Sandra had. There he was, just about to light a cigarette with that confounded lighter. I tried to reason with him, but the man's demands left me fearful that I would be obligated to him and his whims for life. I only pushed him, I never meant to kill him... I didn't even realize I had. I just pushed and he fell back into the water. As he fell, the lighter went up into the air and in a reflex I caught it. I only took it because I thought it would serve him right and make him see my side of things. He never went anywhere without that lighter and I intended to return it."

"You just confessed to murder," Melody said.

"No, I didn't know, I swear I didn't mean to kill him." Richard tried to reach out to Alvin but couldn't with his hands cuffed. "You have to believe me, please!"

"That one's for the DA to decide," Alvin said.

Wilbur read him his rights and was about to lead him away, but there was another question that Melody wanted an answer to. "What about Kirsten?"

A defeated Richard turned his eyes to her and shrugged. "Victor did alter her grades, however, from what I can gather she had nothing to do with it. I did like the Reids and we just wanted to keep it quiet. I guess I was still hoping to receive the donation for the school."

"What will happen to Kirsten?" Melody asked.

"Now that Victor is gone, there is no proof that her grades were altered. I don't think she needs to be brought into this, I think she suffered enough," Richard said.

Melody nodded, she was pleased that the girl would be left out of this. Somehow, she didn't think the boost in her grades would make much difference. Hopefully, Kirsten's parents would allow her to live the life she wanted and not force her to go to college.

Wilbur led Jeffries away and Melody and Alvin were alone in the shop with Smudge. Melody pointed at the profiteroles on the floor and told Smudge to get them. After all, once again she had solved the crime and she deserved a treat to celebrate.

The little dog gave a yip of delight before pouncing on the sweet treat.

"Any more of those profiteroles?" Alvin asked.

"Sorry, my love, Smudge just had the last of them."

Melody couldn't help but chuckle at Alvin's sad face as he watched the bulldog lap up the last of the delicious treat.

CHAPTER TWELVE

It was about a week later and Melody was working in the back of the shop. As usual, Smudge was curled up on her pink furry bed with a green squeaky frog. It would soon be closing time but Melody was trying out a new recipe for a party they had next week. The guests wanted something special and when they gave her the specifications it made Melody smile. It gave her an idea of a way to treat Alvin and that always made her happy.

"How's it coming along?" Leslie asked as she continued on her last batch of cookies.

"I think they will be perfect," Melody said.

"That seems an awful lot of profiteroles for a test," Kerry said as she came into the kitchen after serving a customer. "I think you've got a little bit carried away there, Melody."

Melody paused from cutting the profiteroles and held up her hand. "I think it's the perfect amount of profiteroles for a test… and three double portions, don't you?"

Kerry let out a yelp of joy. "You are just the best boss ever, have I ever told you that, I need to tell you more often, don't you just agree, Leslie, she is the best boss ever…"

"Ker!" Leslie shouted to stop the flow of words. "I do agree."

"But I'm not your boss anymore," Melody said, "remember we are partners. I wanted to treat Alvin, he's been in a little sulk since Smudge ate all the profiteroles when he came to rescue me. I thought this new recipe would be just perfect as a treat for him, and if I'm going to treat him why shouldn't I treat you two and your wonderful partners?"

"Sounds great to me," Leslie said. "You need any help?"

"I can help too," Kerry said. "Everything is put away and we'll be closing in fifteen minutes."

"I've mixed up all the cream, why don't you start piping and I'll work on the caramel sauce," Melody said as she crossed to the stove.

"This cream smells gorgeous," Leslie said sneaking a little taste. "Is this rum?"

"Rum!" Kerry said and then took a taste herself but not quite as sneakily. "Oh, my, it's delicious."

Melody laughed at her two partners. "It's a good job this batch is for us, with all those fingers going in the cream."

Leslie and Kerry looked suitably bashful as Melody worked on the caramel sauce.

"Yes, it's rum, for the Booths' party next week. They wanted something a little special. When I asked about their favorites this seemed perfect. I'm going to save a few of them as a taster and the rest are all for us.

The three partners worked together in silence. Kerry and Leslie made a good team as they filled the choux balls and placed them in four containers. Just as

Melody finished the sauce the bell to the shop tinkled. Leslie was the one with her hands free so she went through while the other two ladies continued working.

The smell of the caramel sauce over the rum was delightful. Melody was really pleased with the new recipe. She knew that Alvin was going to be buzzed by this, and she couldn't wait to share it with him. Once everything was done, they just had to wait for the sauce to cool before the lids could be fitted and they could take them home.

"It's Mr. and Mrs. Reid and Kirsten for you," Leslie called.

Melody felt a flutter of panic in her stomach. It was partly her fault that it had been found out about Kirsten's grades irregularity. Even though the principal had said he wouldn't release the information, it had somehow got out and Melody wondered just what the Reids wanted to say to her. Would they be angry? It didn't matter, she had to face them and as she went to the door to the shop she noticed that Smudge was there before her. *Good!* It didn't hurt to have a little bit of support.

"Mr. and Mrs. Reid, Kirsten, how can I help you?" Melody asked putting on her brightest smile.

It was Sandra that spoke, which surprised Melody a little bit. In the past, she had often deferred to her husband. Maybe this was a change for the good.

"We wanted to thank you for your help," Sandra said. "Oh, and please call us Sandra and Franklin. We are so relieved that the real killer was found, even if the death was an accident and we have an apology to make." Her head dropped and she rung her hands together in front of her.

"No, you have nothing to apologize for," Melody said.

Smudge had gone under the counter and was rubbing her head against Sandra's leg offering her support.

"Sandra is right," Franklin said. "We not only owe you an apology, for we thought you and your husband were meddling... now we understand that you were simply following the leads and that nothing was personal. Most of all, we want you to know how sorry we are for the way we pushed Kirsten."

Kirsten was nodding her head and Melody realized now that she looked so much more relaxed. In the past, the girl had always appeared to be walking on eggshells. Her head was always bowed, her eyes furtive, and she kept away from her parents as much as possible. The Kirsten before them was a confident, happy teenager and it made Melody's heart swell to see it.

"We put too much pressure on our daughter," Sandra said. "What we expected of her was what we wanted and not what she wanted. After speaking to yourself, Kirsten was able to open up to us and let us know it wasn't her dream to go to college. We feel awful for what we put her through."

"No, Mom, you never meant it, you just didn't understand," Kirsten said. "It was partly my fault too, I should've told you I hated the thought of college. I should've told you what I really wanted to do."

"What do you want to do?" Melody asked.

A big smile came over Kirsten's face. "I want to be a mechanic and I've already got an apprenticeship organized. I just love working on engines and seeing how things work."

Melody had not expected that. She glanced at Kirsten's parents and was surprised to see that their faces were full of pride.

"That is wonderful," Melody said. "I know you will make a fabulous mechanic and I hope you'll be very happy."

"Thank you." Kirsten blushed a little at the compliment.

"For now," Sandra said, "we are going away for a few weeks just to let things settle down. We just wanted to drop in and let you know that there are no hard feelings between us before we left. Once we come back, you must let Smudge come over and have a play date with Elvis."

At the mention of her name, Smudge spun in a circle and then gave a big yip.

"I want to wish you all the best of luck," Melody said as her fingers were drawn to her belly. "Family is so important."

"Yes, it is," Franklin said as he put his arm around his daughter and wife and together, as a family, they left the shop.

Melody watched them go and vowed that she and Alvin would always listen to whatever their own son or daughter wanted. They would not try to force their own views on them.

Melody pulled into the drive to see that the lights were on and she could see Alvin working in the kitchen. She hoped he hadn't planned anything for dessert. She picked up the packet of profiteroles before unhooking Smudge from her harness. The little bulldog jumped over her knees, out of the car and ran to the front door. There she gave a little bark.

Alvin opened the door almost instantly and pulled the little Frenchie into a hug. Spinning her around he came down and kissed Melody on the cheek.

"How are you today?" Alvin asked.

"It was interesting," Melody said thinking that she must tell him about the Reids before the night was through.

"Oooh, what have you got there?" Alvin said as he

took the package from her hands and peered inside. "Profiteroles, for me?"

Melody laughed as she took Smudge from his arms and took her into the house. "Not even you could eat all that portion."

"Want to bet?" Alvin winked as he popped the box into the fridge.

Together they finished off preparing the meal and then sat down. As always Alvin served Melody and then put Smudge's bowl down for her before sitting down himself. Today, Alvin had made meatloaf and it was delicious. Melody loved to cook but she sure appreciated coming home to a delicious home-cooked meal.

Together they ate and talked and Melody explained all about the Reids and their hopes for the future.

"It will be great to have a female mechanic," Alvin said. "I know that Joe's Garage was hoping to take a lady on. This will be fabulous.

Once they had eaten and the dishes were cleared away, Melody, Alvin, and Smudge all settled down on the sofa. It was lovely to just relax and talk and

Melody snuggled up against Alvin's shoulder, with Smudge laid across the both of them.

"We must never do that with our kid," Alvin said.

"What?" Melody asked drowsily as she felt his hand drift to her belly and the promise it held there.

Alvin's hand covered hers. "We must never put too much pressure on our little princess," Alvin said. "Never try to make them what we want them to be. We must encourage her..."

"Or him," Melody added quickly.

"Or him, to do what they want to do, no matter what it is. We must let them be the person they want to be."

"I know," Melody said, her other hand now on top of Alvin's. "I've been thinking about it a lot. There are so many things I want our child to be and to do... but we will let them be themselves most of all. Whatever they do, be, or become we will love and support them, promise me."

"I promise," he said before sneaking a kiss of her lips. "There is just one thing that they absolutely have to do."

"Alvin, we can't say that..."

"Oh, yes we can, they have to love dogs... or at least one dog."

Smudge stood up and kissed his cheek before giving her own yip of agreement.

Melody could agree with that one, after all, who wouldn't love Smudge?

If you enjoyed this book Grab Smudge and the Stolen Puppies FREE when you join my newsletter here

Read on for an amazing offer

I now have 2 fabulous box sets for you to enjoy. The first box set is the first 6 books in this cute mystery series with the best French Bulldog ever! Grab the first 6 books in the Bakers and Bulldogs series in this box set for FREE with Kindle Unlimited here

Now here is a preview of the 2nd box set with books 7 to 12

The morning was bright and cheery, and the last remnants of winter had finally left the cozy little seaside town of Port Warren. Melody had gotten up nice and early and was ready for the day ahead.

In the kitchen, a little bundle of joy bounced up and down on all four paws. Called a blue and white, because her dark grey coat looked blue, Smudge was happy to be moving. Melody snapped the leash onto the faithful puppy's collar, and the pair set off to work.

Taking the scenic route, she and Smudge had sauntered along, basking in all of the sights and sounds that the first days of spring had to offer. The snow had finally melted, tiny green shoots could be found pushing their way up through the fresh earth, and a few birds had made their return from down south and were gleefully singing their morning songs. Smudge pranced along ahead, tail wagging, leading the way to Decadently Delicious. This was the award-winning bakery that Melody had opened a few years earlier. Being the skilled pastry chef that she was, it was no surprise that the bakery was thriving. New orders came in daily, and there was always a steady stream of people coming and going, picking up their favorite desserts to bring home for a tasty after-dinner treat.

Fumbling with her keys, Melody unlocked the front door to the shop, stepped inside and switched on the lights, ready to get to work. She went back to the kitchen, turned on all of the ovens, and did a quick inventory check to ensure that all of the necessary supplies and ingredients were on hand to fulfill the day's orders. Everything was set and ready to go. The only things missing were her two assistants. As she pulled up her sleeve to check her watch, she heard the front door chimes ring. Seconds later, Kerry Porter, her first assistant came bouncing into the back.

"You'll never guess what I did last night, Mel!" Kerry started in her normal exuberant way. She always spoke so fast that no one could get a word in edgeways. It looked like this morning was no exception. "It was absolutely wonderful! Bradford took me out for the most romantic dinner at the new steakhouse downtown, and then after dinner we spent the rest of the evening dancing. We spun around the room in each other's arms. It was absolutely magical!" Kerry was swooning and pretending to dance around the shop. It seemed that her relationship with Bradford was recovering nicely from some of the hardships that it had gone through in its early days.

Melody laughed. "I'm really happy for you, Ker. I'm so glad that after all that you and Bradford have been through, things are finally working out. Just remember," she gestured to her watch, tapping its glass face, "I can't have you letting your personal relationships get in the way of work. You're ten minutes late already. We could have had the first batch of cakes mixed and ready to go into the oven by now."

Nodding at Melody, Kerry agreed. "You're totally right, Mel, I'm really sorry. I got off to a late start this morning. I swear it will never happen again." Kerry took a quick look around. "At least I'm here earlier than Leslie. Where is she anyway? It's not like her to be this tardy."

"Your right, Kerry, she is usually pretty punctual." Melody sighed, where was that girl? "We have a ton of orders to complete today. I'd better give her a call and find out what's going on."

Melody pulled out her cell phone and dialed Leslie's number, but there was no answer. Hanging up she tried again, and again. Finally, with no joy, she left a message for Leslie to return her call or come into the bakery as soon as possible. Melody turned to Kerry. "No answer," she said. "It's strange, but I'm sure she will show up. We'd better not waste any more time, or else no one will be getting their treats today."

Halfway through their second batch of double chocolate fudge cupcakes, Leslie came running in, startling Smudge out of a quick nap and causing the pup to start up into a round of barking. The girl was out of breath and had apparently run the whole way from her home to the bakeshop.

Kerry put a hand on Smudge's head to reassure her and to bring some calm to the chaotic situation that Leslie had created. "Well, good morning!" Kerry joked, considering it was nearly the afternoon. "Where have you been? We've been here slaving away, trying to pick up your slack."

"I'm so sorry, guys," Leslie apologized, looking sincerely upset.

Melody walked over, wiping her hands on her apron, and was interested to hear what kind of excuse Leslie had for her late arrival.

Leslie looked a little embarrassed but sort of glowing

at the same time. "I actually think I have a new calling, guys! I mean, don't get me wrong, I'll never give up baking, but I met someone yesterday afternoon, and he's opened up my eyes to a whole new world of possibilities!"

Melody and Kerry looked at each other quizzically and then back at Leslie, waiting for her to continue.

"I was at the market, picking up some groceries when I dropped an orange. It rolled away, down the aisle, and as I was chasing it, I bumped right into Jamison Shepherd. He's from New York, and he's acting as the guest director for the Port Warren playhouse. He has been involved in so many productions with plenty of famous actors and actresses, and he has a ton of amazing stories." Leslie clasped her hands together and closed her eyes as if reliving the meeting. "We hit it off right away. We went out for a few drinks and then dinner and ended up staying up almost all night discussing writing and art and the meaning of life." Leslie had a faraway look in her eyes as she spoke.

"I see," Kerry said, trying to hide the smirk on her face. "So, you're in love? You've got the hots for this fancy new director?"

Leslie's face turned bright red at Kerry's remarks. "No!" She exclaimed, perhaps a little too loudly. "It's not like that. I mean, he's a great guy and all, but I'm just really looking forward to auditioning for the play. Jamison thinks I'll make a great actress."

"I think that's really nice, Leslie," Melody said, putting a hand on the girl's shoulder. "You're going to have a wonderful time, but you have to make sure that you keep your priorities straight and get to work on time. We need your help here. Also, be careful of this Jamison guy. He's new to town and comes from the big city. Things are a lot different out there. Make sure you keep your head about you until you get to know him a little better. You never know what someone's intentions may be."

Leslie vowed that she would be vigilant on both fronts. "I won't be late again, Mel, this was a one-time mistake, I swear. I'll be careful of Jamison as well, but I promise you, he's a really great guy, you guys are going to adore him!" And with that she quickly threw on an apron and set to work, baking up a batch of macaroons.

Melody shook her head and sighed, setting off

towards her office with Smudge at her heels. There was never a dull moment at Decadently Delicious.

Grab this amazing value set for free here

To be the first to find out when Rosie releases a new book and to hear about other sweet romance authors join the exclusive SweetBookHub readers club here.

Bakers and Bulldogs Cozy Mystery Series:

Cupcakes and Crimes volume 1 - 6 Book Box Set

Cupcakes and Crimes volume 2 - 6 Book Box Set

Kidnapped at the Casino

Murder and the Magician

Wedding Dresses and Deadly Messes

Dying to Retire

The Stylist and the Deadly Cut

The Murder in the Motel

If you enjoyed this book, Rosie would appreciate it if you
left a review on Amazon or Goodreads.

This little bundle of Frenchie love would appreciate it too,
this is Lila, also known as Piggy Pig.